STICKS AND STONES, BOBBIE BONES

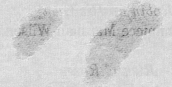

Other Apple Paperbacks
you will enjoy:

Afternoon of the Elves
by Janet Taylor Lisle

Cousins
by Virginia Hamilton

Eenie, Meenie, Murphy, NO!
by Colleen O'Shaughnessy McKenna

Robin on His Own
by Johnniece Marshall Wilson

Risk n' Roses
by Jan Slepian

STICKS AND STONES, BOBBIE BONES

Brenda C. Roberts

AN
APPLE
PAPERBACK

SCHOLASTIC INC.
New York Toronto London Auckland Sydney

No part of this publication may be reproduced in whole or in part, or stored in a retrieval system, or transmitted in any form or by any means, electronic, mechanical, photocopying, recording, or otherwise, without written permission of the publisher. For information regarding permission, write to Scholastic Inc., 730 Broadway, New York, NY 10003.

ISBN 0-590-46518-X

12 11 10 9 8 7 6 5 4   4 5 6 7 8/9

Printed in the U.S.A.   40

First Scholastic printing, January 1993

155487

For Gisele and Hayley,
Virgil P., Loubertha,
Carol, and all my family

STICKS AND STONES, BOBBIE BONES

1

Maybe today would be a good day. She lay
very still, listening. The morning had a
friendly sound. The birds were hitting their high
notes. A breeze was nudging sleepy trees, leaf
waking leaf in soft green rustling. Things sounded
promising.

But you never could tell so early in the day.
You had to be at least halfway through it before
you could tell if you had a blockbuster, class "A"
day, or just another loser.

Lately, Bobbie had been having a streak of
losers.

There were the days when Mrs. Schnurr
beamed brightly at her. "Come up here to the
chalkboard, Bobbie," she would chirp. "Show
everyone how to solve this."

All eyes on her, Bobbie would creep up to the
board and solve the problem with a few quick
strokes. The other kids thought this was cool —

like Florida in the summer, it was cool.

There were also loser days when she was tense and miserable because of Myra Collins. Myra was fond of hissing nicknames at her, like "Bobbie Bones" and "Scrambled Egghead." Charming, that Myra. Reminded Bobbie of something that coils and rattles before striking.

Then there were the days — every day, in fact — when she looked up at recess and found herself all alone.

And days when Isaac looked straight through her.

Those kinds of days.

Bobbie sighed a last lingering sigh before kicking back the blanket and swinging her feet down to the floor, thinking, *The odds are with me. I've had eight rotten days in a row. I'm eight for eight. I'm due for a really good one.*

Even so, she automatically started to calculate what time she'd have to be past the school gate to avoid tall, taunting Myra.

"This is ridiculous," she scolded herself. "Two months at this school and I'm still sneaking in. What am I, anyway? A mouse? Am I some kind of . . . of . . . loser?"

She refused to answer herself. Instead, she darted into the bathroom, quickly washed, and shoved on her rather thick glasses. Then she returned to the bedroom and began her morning ritual: substituting something for every single item her mother had laid out the night before.

For the "precious" red sweater from Aunt Mave, appliquéd with buttercups and forget-me-nots: a gray sweatshirt. For the navy blue woolen skirt pinched into a thousand and one "darling" eenie-weenie pleats: black leggings. For the red tights, also sent by her clucking Aunt Mave: big white socks. Next came the sneakers, and the ritual was complete.

Bobbie stood on her bed to check herself out in the dresser mirror. "Better!" she breathed.

She thought back to her first day at the new school, when she'd let her mother convince her to wear that "precious" sweater and that "darling" skirt. She'd felt like the original Miss Priss: stiff, stuffy, and hopelessly out of it.

What she saw in the mirror this morning was no Miss Universe, but no Miss Priss, either. She saw clear, dark brown skin: a plus. Thick black hair roped into twin ponytails on either side of her head: another plus. A ten-going-on-eleven body that looked more like seven-going-on-eight: a minus, she admitted.

Her large, bright, candid brown eyes usually stole the show from the rest of her face. Some people never even noticed her glasses at first. So the eyes were definitely a plus.

In all, it was a pretty good reflection staring

back at her from the mirror. With her hopeful expression and her chin up, she looked to herself like someone people would like to know. To have as a pal. So what was the problem?

Bobbie tried a couple of "Like Me" smiles in the mirror before her eyes fell on her mother's little clock on the dresser, second hand racing round its face. She jumped down from the bed, quickly snapped the sheets into place, and looked around the room.

She and her mother shared the bedroom. "Kind of like roommates," Mrs. Ruffin had smiled when they moved in. Bobbie had known her mother was trying her best to be cheerful about things, so she had smiled along with her. Before the divorce, Bobbie had had her own room.

She did miss spreading her things out all over, her floor-to-ceiling posters, the big shaggy tangerine-colored rug she used to sprawl on after school. It was obvious there would be no room for her rug in this small room. Her mom had sold it in a garage sale at their old house, right before they'd moved.

Now they had twin beds with matching yellow spreads, and Mrs. Ruffin had stitched curtains out of the same sunny fabric.

Bobbie's bed was usually crowded with her critters, which she had stuffed and sewn up using gingham, fake fur, whatever she had at hand. Her books were stashed in boxes beneath the bed and on the shelf next to it. Pictures and postcards, some from her dad and some from Aunt Mave, covered up most of the space remaining.

Mrs. Ruffin's side of the room looked stripped by comparison. Her bed was bare except for a round emerald-green pillow, a birthday gift from Bobbie, who had embroidered "Give It A Rest" in its middle. The thread had worked its way loose on one side, and now it commanded mysteriously: "Give It A R---."

Anyway, her mother didn't crowd her too much. Mrs. Ruffin spent most of her hours at the kitchen table, laboring over schoolwork. At the high school where she'd been hired as a history teacher, the principal had "a difficult personality," Mrs. Ruffin had told Bobbie. So she was always sitting up late with lesson plans and essays. "Can't afford to give old Wigfall an excuse to nag," she would explain with a sleepy-looking grin.

"Bobbie! Breakfast!" Mrs. Ruffin called now from the kitchen.

"Coming!" Bobbie answered hastily, shifting into a higher gear. Out of habit, she pushed her glasses up on her nose, and headed out.

"Roberta Mavis Ruffin." Her mother's voice was tired. "This switching clothes thing is really getting to be a habit with you, kiddo."

Bobbie breezed past Mrs. Ruffin and climbed

onto the stool at the counter. "Momma, those clothes are too hot. And the sweater scratches my arms," she complained.

Mrs. Ruffin folded her arms. "Uh-huh," she nodded skeptically. "And I guess that sweatshirt is nice and cool, huh?"

She went back to stirring the hot cereal, her black hair smoothed back, her crisp, white shirt tucked under her suit jacket. A few worry lines had worked their way across her brow over the past year. The divorce, the move, the new job, the late hours, had all done their bit.

But her face was still full of humor most of the time. She even managed to pull off a few wise-cracks most mornings. Not too many this morning, though; last night had been a long haul.

"Hey, look," she explained, a note of irritation in her voice. "Your Aunt Mave pays good money for those clothes. It gives her a kick to send you things."

Bobbie felt an attitude coming on. "Baby things!" she muttered. "Why can't she just send the money? I can pick out better clothes than she can."

"I've never asked Mave to send me money and don't plan to start now. If she's sweet enough to send presents to a girl who pokes her lip out and rolls her eyes at people, then that's up to her." Mrs. Ruffin took a swig of pitch black wake-me,

6

shake-me coffee and arched an eyebrow. "Now gobble down that cereal, child of mine. We'll be late again."

Glowering, Bobbie began to stir her cereal. "If you dress like a baby," she grumbled to nobody, "people treat you like a baby."

"I said *eat*, Buster," her mother repeated. Bobbie shoveled a too-hot spoonful of cereal into her mouth and rolled it around on her tongue, sucking in air to cool it off.

"Besides," her mother added, "people only treat you like a baby if you *act* like a baby. Chapter One, Mother's Book of Wisdom."

Easy for you *to say*, Bobbie said. But she said it to herself.

She made short work of her cereal — she had a weakness for Cream of Wheat. And she made good time gathering her things. But when the clock said it was time to go, Bobbie came up with ten good reasons why she couldn't. Her sneaker laces had come undone. Her hair wasn't right. She couldn't find her homework log.

"You'll never get to school at this rate, kiddo." Slim and cocoa-brown, Mrs. Ruffin stood at the door, glasses neat on her nose.

Duh, Bobbie thought. Aloud, she just said, "I'm going, I'm going."

Mrs. Ruffin tapped her foot while Bobbie tied and retied her shoelaces with painstaking precision. "Okay, what's the matter?" she asked finally. "First you give me grief about Aunt Mave, and now you suddenly forget how to tie your shoes!"

"Nothing's the matter."

"Oh, yeah?"

"Yeah."

Mrs. Ruffin looked at her daughter closely. "Well, something's going on. Every day it's taking you longer and longer to get out of here. Is it something about school?"

Bobbie turned her face away from her mother and half-swallowed her answer: "Not actually."

Mrs. Ruffin's face was still for a moment. "Not actually?" she echoed.

Bobbie shrugged.

"Okay, honey," Mrs. Ruffin said with a sigh, glancing at her watch. She had described to Bobbie how Mr. Wigfall patrolled the hall every morning with his pocket watch in his hand, his sour old mug spoiling the day for everyone.

"We'll talk about it later," she said. "Now step on it, girl, so I can lock up! I have to be on time today."

Bobbie dragged her feet out the door and headed east, stopping once to pull up her socks. Looking back, she saw Mrs. Ruffin heading west. Her slender form tilted forward as she strode along, as if she were trying to get out in front of time itself.

Watching her turn the corner, Bobbie had an attack of the guilties. She hoped she hadn't made her mother late again.

It hadn't been easy for Bobbie, moving to a new school in a new town. But for now, she figured she'd keep this trouble with Myra to herself. *Momma's got enough problems*, she thought, her mind on Mr. Wigfall. *Wish I could do something . . .*

She pictured herself in a sharp green and gold Spandex costume, her cape billowing behind her as she soared above the high school where Mrs. Ruffin taught. Spying Mr. Wigfall's bald, shiny head, she saw herself swoop down and scoop him up. For the next three blocks, she amused herself by imagining the principal struggling in her clutches.

Just as she was about to decide his fate, her own school came in sight and her daydream dissolved.

"Boy," Bobbie sighed. "Back to reality." Adjusting her heavy book bag, she walked slowly into the waiting jaws of Lowell Elementary.

2

Good fortune or good figuring got Bobbie past the school gate without incident. Myra Collins and her sidekicks had already gone inside the old brick building. Bobbie's spirits fluttered hopefully. Maybe this was going to be one of those rare, blessed, peaceful days.

The bell had barely rung when it became clear just how peaceful it would be.

"Pop quiz!"

Mrs. Schnurr was very fond of pop quizzes. But they were the bane of Bobbie's life. Not that she didn't do well on them, which she did. That part was good. It was just that Mrs. Schnurr loved to broadcast the results. That part was bad.

It was bad because Bobbie's name always sat on or near the top of the scale, and Myra's rarely inched past the lowest third percentile. It didn't take a megabrain to see how this affected Myra. Once, after a test, she broke her No. 2 pencil clean in two. Another time, she twisted her quiz paper into a hangman's noose. So whenever Mrs. Schnurr twittered "Pop quiz!" Bobbie wished she could temporarily evaporate from the face of the earth.

"Another day in the trash can," she moped. She was sure of it when the teacher stopped in front of her table and smiled her small, careful smile.

"Bobbie, I want you and Isaac to help me grade the math quizzes today," she said, her little pointed chin sticking out over her high stiff collar.

The girl felt all eyes on the back of her neck. But Mrs. Schnurr was oblivious. Turning to the other students, she enunciated crisply. "I won't be announcing any grades aloud today, class. That should make a few of you very happy."

She tittered at her little joke. She was always tittering at her little jokes.

After twice repeating instructions about the quiz and ignoring the usual wave of grumbles, Mrs. Schnurr handed out the test papers. As expected, Bobbie and Isaac finished first and gave their papers to the teacher for grading. Then they sat down at the table in front, squeezed in between Mrs. Schnurr's beloved ant farms and cacti.

Bobbie could barely breathe with Isaac so near.

Looking at him was out of the question, but she didn't really need to look. She'd had him pretty well memorized since her first week at Lowell.

He was the tallest boy in the class, and the leanest. So lean, in fact, that his hands and feet looked . . . just . . . gigantic. Especially those feet. It was phenomenal, Bobbie thought, how he could make feet like that work together so well on the basketball court. Or when he was just plain walking, for that matter. But she and the rest of Lowell Elementary kept their opinions to themselves about Isaac's feet. He was just a little sensitive on that subject.

Anyway, his feet had nothing to do with his mind. The boy's brain, as Mrs. Schnurr had been overheard to say, was "as nimble as a brand new needle." Meaning he was very, very smart. And he knew it well. So well that the word "conceited" seemed fair, even to Bobbie.

But, like everyone else, she forgave him that. After all, he wasn't obnoxious about it. He just accepted it as a fact of life and expected the world to accept it, too.

Isaac had rich Hershey's chocolate skin, and Bobbie imagined that his eyes were a deep, brooding brown to match. She had never actually seen them. He wore triple-thickness lenses in his eyeglasses, kept strapped to his head by a tight black elastic band. Without those glasses, he might as well hang it up.

But that was okay, too. Everything about him was okay with Bobbie. Extremely okay. And here he was, only inches away.

And there was Myra, in the back row, narrow snake eyes watching their every move.

Bobbie knew Myra Collins considered Isaac her personal territory. She also knew that Myra Collins did not take it kindly when Bobbie or any other girl sat anywhere near Isaac. And, she also knew how Myra felt about skinny girls who wore glasses and thought they were *so* smart.

Wiping perspiration off her nose, Bobbie could almost hear Myra's blood boiling. The thought of it made her feel queasy.

If only Myra were a flat-out genius, Bobbie sighed. Then she wouldn't have time for a certain wonderful, conceited boy with big feet. Or time to worry about girls with skinny legs and too many brains.

On Bobbie's first day at Lowell, she had self-consciously tiptoed to the seat Mrs. Schnurr had pointed out to her. Past rows of strange eyes. In her "precious" little flower-dotted sweater, that pinch-pleat skirt, and those baggy red tights.

Shrinking under all the curious eyes, she had begun plotting how she could intercept the next package from good old Aunt Mave. And then she heard it:

"Don't rub 'em together, girl. They might catch on fire."

Bobbie had stopped, mystified. She had looked down and suddenly seen how very red, how fire-engine red her legs must have looked in her sagging tights on that gray fall morning. Mortified, she'd looked up and seen Myra's smirk for the first time. It was not a pretty sight.

Disoriented, Bobbie had desperately searched for her seat. After forever and a minute, she found it, collapsed into it, and pushed her glasses up on her nose.

Myra was actually not a bad-looking girl, if you didn't mind large. She had been born "big-boned," as old people called it, but she had curly jet-black hair and perfect posture when she felt like it. Without her scowl, she would be considered quite pretty.

But few people had ever seen Myra's face clean of that scowl. It came with the package, Bobbie guessed.

She imagined she would have escaped Myra's notice altogether except for one thing: her brain. If anything made Myra mad, it was people with brains — except for Isaac, of course. Isaac was *always* the exception.

Bobbie had often wondered about Myra's dislike

for people with brains, until Back to School Night. That was when she first saw Myra's parents in action. Mr. Collins had thumbed through the work in Myra's folder, scrunched up his face, and shaken his head tragically. Mrs. Collins went around, checked out all the other folders, and came back to Myra with jaws tight as a drum. Then they'd started giving it to poor Myra left and right, *dit-dit-dit* in both ears.

It was enough to make a person sorry — even for Myra Collins. But why does she take it out on me?, Bobbie argued. What am I supposed to do, play dumb?

Her thoughts were interrupted by a sneaky-looking girl from the front row, who tossed a crumpled ball of paper at her as soon as Mrs. Schnurr's back was turned. In slow motion, Bobbie smoothed out the note and held her breath. "Oh no," she exhaled. It was from Myra. The note said:

If you get my test,
you no what to do

Bobbie shuddered. The way her day was going, she had no doubt that she would wind up with Myra's test.

After an eternity of pencil-biting and feet shuf-

15

fling, the last of the students surrendered their papers to Mrs. Schnurr. Pursing her lips sensibly, the teacher shuffled all the papers, gave half to Isaac and half to Bobbie. Then she handed them the key paper. "You'll have to share the key. Get closer together so you can both see it."

Bobbie wondered why Mrs. Schnurr was so determined to get her killed.

3

The next twenty minutes were nearly intoler-
able, what with Bobbie's heart thundering
and her head throbbing. Or vice versa. She could
hardly hear Mrs. Schnurr squawking away about
fractions and decimal points, her heels clicking as
she paced in front of the class.

Isaac had already finished three or four quizzes
before Bobbie got a grip on herself and began.
She worked her way through the first five papers.
So far, so good. And then . . . bingo. There it was.
Myra's test.

Why me? she heard a small, small voice murmur
inside her head.

Sweat dampened her hands and underarms.
Her glasses slid down her nose; she pushed them
up anxiously. She stole a look at Myra, who had
a dagger waiting deep in one eye, glittering.

In a panic, Bobbie decided to save herself.

Mrs. Schnurr seldom rechecked her scoring, she

reminded herself. Mrs. Schnurr trusted her work. And, after all, her skin was at risk. Didn't she owe it to her skin to look out for it?

Maybe it wouldn't be so bad, she reasoned. Maybe Myra had lucked up on some right answers for a change. Desperately, she scanned the sheet. Her heart sank way down in her chest. Wrong, wrong, wrong. The paper was riddled with wrong answers.

Bobbie felt up against it. She was sure she would never know another peaceful moment if she sent Myra's test back with the score it deserved.

Isaac was working quickly; he would finish soon. She was going to have to do it now. Just a few token red checks would be enough. She didn't have to give Myra a top score. For Myra, something like 70%, even 60%, would be a major achievement.

Do it, Bobbie's skin begged. *Save me!*

She wanted to do it. The threat of Myra Collins was fairly vibrating in the air. Her hand gripped the red pen. Just a few little checks and she and her skin would get out of there in one piece. Mrs. Schnurr would never know.

The red pen was poised. Bobbie was breathing so hard she started to hiccup. The pen descended. Bobbie willed her hand to obey, willed it with all her might.

"Please," she whined under her hiccups. "Please think about the rest of this body."

But the hand wouldn't budge. She realized sadly that, come what may, she was to be known as Miss Priss to the bitter end. And, as Miss Priss, her fate was sealed.

Mechanically, dutifully, her red pen found each wrong answer and struck.

4

As the quiz papers were returned to the class, Bobbie wondered if she were still visible. She felt as if she'd sweated away to nothing. After a quick look at Myra, who was staring unhappily at the red "28%" marked on her test, she felt positively liquified. Big drops began to dribble from her armpits down her sides into the fold of her fleecy top.

Thank the Lord for sweatshirts, she thought miserably.

Clicking back and forth in front of the classroom, Mrs. Schnurr allowed her students a few minutes to look over the quiz papers.

Then, in the high twitter that reached even the seats in the back, she began to lecture them about "effort" and "determination" and "logic."

"Think of mathematics as your friend," she was saying.

"Some friend!" quipped Roland, a jolly boy in

the back row, loudly enough for his buddies to hear. They snorted in appreciation, but Mrs. Schnurr did not notice. She was on a roll, enjoying her little speech.

"Think of numbers as your little helpers," she suggested smugly.

Roland groaned and, turning so that only his back row buddies could see, pretended to lose his breakfast on the hardwood floor. He clutched his middle and rolled his eyes, writhing, muffling his laughter.

This time, Mrs. Schnurr caught Roland's act, but she did not titter along with the back row. Mrs. Schnurr only tittered at her own little jokes. At the moment, she was not amused.

Her face was pinched as she clicked down the narrow aisle to Roland's desk. She stopped in front of him and watched stonily as he tried to stifle his last few giggles.

"Is your stomach upset, Mr. Lemmon?" she demanded. Mrs. Schnurr always used one's last name when one was in trouble.

Roland peeked at her pinched-up face. Before he could answer, a fresh cascade of giggles gushed up and out. The more his chubby body shook, the more the class whooped.

Mrs. Schnurr did not approve. Drawing herself up like a parakeet drill sergeant, she commanded, "Up, if you please, Mr. Lemmon."

Roland tumbled out of his seat and struggled to his feet, still tickled.

"MARCH!" The teacher pointed to what she called The Study Booth, what the class called The Pit. It was just a chair which sat near the teacher's desk, away from the main action. But they all hated to sit there. You could do nothing without being seen by everyone, especially by Mrs. Schnurr, who had the voice of a canary but the eyes of an eagle.

Roland collapsed into The Pit, suddenly glum. Mrs. Schnurr faced the class. "Mr. Lemmon needs time to let his tummy settle," she announced, eyeing Roland, who began to squirm.

The commotion was a welcome break for Bobbie, who hoped the quiz results would be forgotten in the swirl of laughter and entertainment.

But no such luck. Another note found its way to her before class was out. She knew what was in this one, and who had sent it. The only unknowns were the time and the place. The second note informed her in thick, scrawled letters:

You have made a bad mistak
I am going to kik your you no what
Affther school at the park

Myra never minced words.

Bobbie thought back to the morning. *Maybe this would be a good day*, she had thought. A good day! If *this* was a good day . . .

What she needed was a hero. On second thought, a friend would do just as well. What in the world was she thinking of, getting herself on Myra's bad side? Was she crazy? She had never even been in a fight — she wouldn't know what to do. And she had no buddies to defend her.

Let's face it, Priss, she leveled with herself. *It looks bad for you. Very, very bad.*

After the final bell, Bobbie inched towards the school gate, taking baby steps. "What a world," she sighed pitifully.

"You'll never get there at that rate, girl."

Bobbie had heard that phrase once too often today. She looked up, surprised.

5

Isaac's face squinted at her from behind his glasses. He had his basketball under his arm. Seeing him so unexpectedly, Bobbie went numb from head to foot. They stood there uncomfortably, in silence, as he shifted the ball from arm to arm.

Finally he spoke again. "What's up? You don't look so good."

Bobbie looked at her shoelaces. She tried to say something. After all, this was Isaac standing there. She ought to say something. But her brain had stalled.

They began to walk. That is, Isaac began to walk and Bobbie fell in step. Clearly, he had intended to trot off to the basketball court, but her manner was so gloomy that he hesitated.

"Where you going?" he asked, to break the silence.

24

Bobbie swallowed hard and blinked back tears. "I haven't made up my mind yet."

Isaac took a sideways look at her. He had heard about the scheduled showdown at the park. "You ain't goin' to the park, are you?" he asked bluntly. "Hey, I wouldn't advise it. Myra will definitely kick your — "

"I know, I know." Bobbie didn't need to hear it again.

"So go home. From what I hear, nobody's expectin' you to show up anyway."

Bobbie stopped. "Nobody. Like who nobody?"

"Like everybody. You know, all those girls that like to hang around. They just want to see a fight. But nobody expects you to actually show up."

"Why not?" The idea of an audience made Bobbie's knees turn to water, but she was curious.

"Hey, come on, girl. You know you don't fight."

His last words got through to her. Roberta "Rocky" Ruffin. What a joke. But admitting it didn't solve her problem. She needed a quick solution. She had never had any kind of real conversation with Isaac before, and here she was about to ask his opinion, as if they had known each other for years. But he did seem concerned in his own way, so maybe he wouldn't mind.

"Isaac," she began, then paused, breathing hard. *Go on*, she thought. *Ask him.*

"Isaac," she began again. "I have to ask you —

what can I say to get me out of this? I mean, I've got to come up with something good."

"Why don't you just go on home? You don't have to say nothin' to nobody." For Isaac, the situation was as simple as that.

"Because then I have to see her tomorrow and the next day and the next day. And sooner or later she'll make another move." That possibility made Bobbie feel nauseous.

They fell silent again. Isaac bounced his ball.

"Well, I can't see you going toe to toe with that big mama. She'd kick your — "

"Isaac, I know, I know."

"Well . . ." He looked towards the basketball court, sighing softly. "Shoot; I was gonna . . ."

He sighed again and looked at Bobbie.

"Well, come on." He elbowed her a little in the direction of the park.

Bobbie's body fluids froze. "We're going over there?"

"May as well get it over with," he said with the air of a general who could handle anything, anytime, anywhere. He ran ahead of her, dribbling the ball. "Come on, I'll take care of this."

Oh man, Bobbie thought, eyes closed in dread. *Why me why me why me why me why me?* She slung her book bag over her shoulder and scurried after him.

The school playground was emptying quickly

and, even under these circumstances, it was nice to have company. Bobbie had forgotten how nice. Since coming to Lowell, that "Snobby Bobbie" label had stuck to her like flypaper; no one ever fell in step with her on the way home.

"Isaac," she gasped, barely keeping pace with his long loping gait.

"Yeah?" He turned and dribbled backwards, unconcerned about what might be behind him.

"Why do the kids here — why is it — they don't seem to —" she stammered. "Why don't they — "

"Why don't they like you?" he finished for her.

She nodded gratefully.

"They like you okay." He expertly bounced the ball under one leg, then another.

"But nobody walks with me or eats with me at lunchtime," Bobbie pointed out between breaths.

"They like you okay," he repeated. "They just don't know you. Besides, you do act kind of snobby, if you wanna know the truth."

"Snobby? I act snobby?" she cried. How in the world could anybody think that?

"First day at school you wouldn't even look at anybody," Isaac said matter-of-factly. "Only person you say anything to is Old Lady Snoot."

"Old Lady Snoot? You mean Mrs. Schnurr?"

"Only in class," Isaac grinned. His grin was nice, even though one incisor crossed halfway over

27

the other. "You ever notice how hard it is to say Schnurr? Shoot, that's why everybody calls her Snoot or Shnurdle or Shnoo."

"I didn't know that. I never heard anybody call her Shnoo."

"They probably figured you'd blab it out." Isaac glanced at Bobbie's mournful face and shrugged. "They figure you're the teacher's pet, so . . ."

"But Mrs. Schnurr likes you, too!" The injustice scraped Bobbie's nerves.

Isaac raised his brows. "Hey, hold up!" he backed up in mock alarm. "Take it easy, Miss *Rober-ta*. They all know me already. They're not worried about me. I started first grade here. You're the stranger."

Bobbie felt confused. She shoved her glasses up to the bridge of her nose, where they slouched, lopsided.

She felt the urge to explain to Isaac that she, of all people, was no snob. Shy, yes. Snob, no. Some people couldn't just take over, like he could. Or make everyone laugh, like Roland. Or intimidate, like Big Myra.

All this teetered on her tongue, but they were nearing the park. It was only a few blocks from Lowell, past the dry cleaners, barber shop, service station, shoe store. Green and mysterious, its trees loomed over the shop roofs.

Seeing it, Bobbie slowed down so much that Isaac had to turn around and dribble back to get her.

"You coming? Come on," he said.

"Are you sure this is a good idea?" she asked, her nerve draining rapidly.

Isaac frowned, a little impatient. "Didn't you just say you had to deal with it? Do you want Myra in your face tomorrow and the next day?"

"No. No. I don't want that. No." Bobbie hadn't known until that second what her tongue tasted like bone dry. There was not a droplet of moisture in her entire mouth.

"Okay then," Isaac replied, squinting at her hard. "So what's it gonna be?"

Bobbie looked the way she felt; petrified. She was silent.

Isaac began to turn back. "Hey, it's up to you . . . I was on my way to shoot a little ball anyway . . ."

Bobbie snatched his basketball and hugged it to her chest. "Deal with it," she said, trying to drum up some courage. "Right."

Isaac gazed at her doubtfully, but with sympathy. "Hey, don't get yourself upset. I told you I'd take care of it. No problem." He retrieved his ball and they crossed the street to the park.

6

As Isaac had predicted, there was a whole party of girls at the park. They were milling around in the spreading green shade of the park oaks. Waiting. It was worse than Bobbie had imagined. And at the center of the little mob was Miss Myra herself, sitting on a picnic table, eating grapes.

A few girls had already begun to leave as Bobbie and Isaac approached, but when the two came near they nudged each other and settled back to watch.

Bobbie could tell that Myra had seen them coming, but the big girl was taking her time about noticing them. Finally, she looked up. It was clear to Bobbie that Myra was not pleased Isaac had come along.

Myra set the grapes aside. When the moment was right and not a minute before, she stood up. Five feet two inches of danger, ready to go. Her fists rested on her hips as she waited, sneakers set firmly in the grass.

Bobbie began to feel dizzy. She was sure she heard a rattler, but it was only the sprinkler system watering nearby.

Silly, giddy thoughts occurred to her, like telling everyone to relax and take it easy and nobody would get hurt. Like sheriffs always say to lynch mobs.

Myra's voice came from a long way off, rumbling around in Bobbie's ears like low thunder. "I see Miss Bones had to bring a baby-sitter with her."

Bobbie's tongue was suddenly sand. She stood and stared at Myra for a long, wordless minute before a voice broke the void.

"I don't see no baby-sitter." Propping one size 13 special-order-black-and-crimson-High-Five-sneaker on top of the picnic table bench, Isaac folded his arms and looked around for the phantom baby-sitter.

Myra did not respond. Instead, she took a step towards Bobbie. Obligingly, Bobbie backed up a step.

"I guess some people ain't so smart out here in the park," Myra observed acidly. "They just smart in the classroom, when they got the teacher there to back 'em up."

Bobbie tasted rust towards the back of her mouth. She had read somewhere that fear tastes

31

like that. *It must be true*, she thought, *because my jaws feel like they're rusted at the hinges*. She could not make a sound.

Myra started to take another step towards Bobbie, but Isaac swiftly swung his foot down from the bench and got between the two girls.

"Okay, Okay," he said in his best referee's voice. "That's enough." He placed an outsized hand on Myra's shoulder and backed her up a bit.

Myra threw off his hand. "Can't *she* talk?" she fumed, nodding in Bobbie's direction. "What's the matter with *her* mouth?"

Rusted shut, Bobbie replied silently.

"Look here, Big Mama —" Isaac began, ready to wrap things up with a bit of superior logic. But at the words "Big Mama," Myra lost it.

"Don't you 'Big Mama' me, Bigfoot!" she barked. "You ain't even in this!"

The crowd of onlookers fell silent. Myra had called Isaac "Bigfoot." No one ever talked about Isaac's feet. Not ever.

Uh-oh, Bobbie thought anxiously, shifting her eyes from Isaac to Myra and back again. This wasn't going well. *It looks like a good time for me to beam up*.

"What was that you called me?" Isaac asked Myra in disbelief, trying to keep his cool in front of all the girls.

"Well you called me 'Big Mama,' " Myra answered indignantly. By now it was obvious to everyone that she wished she could pull back that "B" word. Frustrated, she shot Bobbie a look that said, "Now look what you made me do!"

Bobbie caught the look. *I knew this would come back to me*, she said to herself.

With difficulty, Isaac got a grip on his cool. He seemed to have decided all this was beneath his dignity. "Okay, I'm gonna pretend I didn't even hear that," he said nobly. "Now before things get ugly out here, all of you girls just go home. Includin' *you*, Myra."

Bobbie watched Myra warily. Would the dragon charge or retreat? If Myra came after her now, what would Isaac do? What would *she* do?

After what seemed like mankind's longest minute, Myra grudgingly backed off. Scornfully, she turned her back on the pair of them. Reaching down, she snatched her sweater up from the grass near Bobbie's feet, as if to keep her personal belongings safe from some disease.

With an air of disappointment, the other girls began to gather backpacks and book bags. Clearly nothing was happening this time. They headed slowly across the sweep of lawn leading to the park exit, gradually resuming their chatter and kidding around. A few broke off to play chicken with the sprinkler, shrieking with delight when the water caught them.

Myra was the last to go. She grabbed her grapes and popped one, nonchalantly, into her mouth. "See you later, Miss Bones," she drawled into Bobbie's ear as she brushed by her. "Without your baby-sitter."

Slinging her sweater over her shoulder, she nodded to Isaac and swaggered away.

As the girls disappeared into the waning afternoon, Bobbie exhaled. Feeling returned to her extremities. As her vocal cords relaxed, she even felt the power of speech coming back.

"Well, uh . . . I guess that's the end of that, huh?" she ventured, hoping against hope. She knew her voice sounded like Tweety Bird, but she couldn't help it.

Isaac grinned at her confidently. "I told ya I'd take care of it," he said. "Piece of cake."

Bobbie wished she had his self-assurance. She was grateful that he had come with her, but she knew she was now in it chin-deep.

"Umm . . . Isaac. I . . . you know, do you think you should've called her 'Big Mama'?" Bobbie asked timidly.

Isaac looked at her, puzzled. "What's wrong with that? I was just joking with the girl."

Geez, Bobbie thought.

"Well, maybe she feels about 'Big Mama' the way you feel about . . . you know, about . . ." Bobbie balked at saying the dreaded "B" word.

She sensed she was pushing it already. Isaac was not the kind of guy who liked to be instructed by anybody.

"About what she called me?" Isaac asked, looking as though he'd tasted something nasty.

Bobbie nodded.

Isaac was silent so long Bobbie thought she had blown it. *Thanks a lot for messing up the one friendship you almost had*, she rebuked herself. *Now he'll wish he'd never gotten mixed up with you.*

But Isaac had worked the problem over in his mind. "Yeah, you're probably right," he said simply.

Yes! Bobbie exulted under her breath. She kept her mouth shut from then on, afraid to spoil the high point of her day.

To her surprise, Isaac walked her all the way to her street. She supposed he was on the lookout in case Myra tried a sneak attack.

For most of the way, Bobbie kept her eyes on the sidewalk. She felt antsy, grateful, pleased, and excited, all at the same time.

"This your street?" Isaac asked as they came to a neat little avenue of aging slate-colored apartment houses, their steps spruced up with cherry red and bright green paint.

"Oh. Yes. My building's halfway down the block." She paused, waiting for inspiration. "Do you . . . would you like a . . . glass of water? Or juice? I think we have apple juice." Her glasses slipped down to the tip of her nose.

But Isaac was already retreating. "Aw, nah. Thanks. Gotta roll on." He spun his ball on his index finger and backed away.

Bobbie cleared her throat nervously. Now that her trial was over — for today, anyway — her shyness was back.

"Isaac," she said in a wee voice.

"Yo." His back was to her now.

"See you tomorrow," she called weakly.

Loping into the afternoon, Isaac shrugged his shoulders in reply. "Right," he said into the wind, and was gone.

Bobbie turned towards her building, rubbing her arm. "Well, we made it," she said to her skin. "For now."

7

"So how was it today, sweetheart? I was just going to stretch out and rest my eyes for a minute but I guess I must've been out cold when you got home. You must've been kind of late, though, hmmm?"

Bobbie's mother turned the heat on under a skilletful of oil and began shaking the sense out of a paper bag filled with cut-up chicken, spices, paprika, and flour.

An indecisive rain was coming down, now and again weakly splattering the kitchen window. It was one of those unexpected showers, nothing fancy and not likely to stay long. But it was a welcome surprise for Bobbie; rain outside and warmth inside made her feel cozy. She wished the world could always be this cozy.

She sat at the kitchen table, her social studies homework spread out in front of her. But she was not concentrating on it. Instead, her eyes followed her mother's dinner preparations.

Bobbie knew how to cook certain things, like meatless spaghetti and sometimes tacos, but it took her so long she wound up getting on her own nerves.

Mrs. Ruffin, on the other hand, wasted no time. She shook the chicken in the bag, dropped it piece by piece into the popping hot cooking oil, put the lid on the pan, wiped the counter, wiped her hands, wiped her brow, and sat down neatly at the kitchen table, reaching for the newspaper.

"So what made you late, kiddo?" She peered at her daughter over the rim of the day's news. "Did you stay after to help your teacher?"

Bobbie squirmed. She didn't feel like bringing the whole day back. She felt tired, thinking about it. She got up from the table and lifted the lid of the skillet.

"You want me to turn these over, Momma?" The chicken was still pale under the bubbling oil.

"No way. That chicken's gotta have a tan before it's ready. Sit down here and tell me how things are going at school. How do you like Mrs. Schnurr?"

Flopping back down into her chair, Bobbie fiddled with the sugar bowl. "She's okay." More fidgeting. "The kids call her the Shnoo."

"The Shnoo?" Mrs. Ruffin tried to keep from

chuckling. "Well, how about the kids? How do you like them? Are they nice?"

"They're okay."

"Just okay?"

"They're all right. I mean, just . . . I still don't know most of them, Momma; I've only been there two months."

Mrs. Ruffin waited.

"They think I'm a brain," Bobbie continued, reluctant. "I think they think Mrs. Schnurr thinks I'm the top brain. Or at least one of the top two brains in there."

"Who's the other brain?"

"Well, there's this boy, Isaac. He wears glasses, too. He's a little bit . . . you know . . . conceited, I guess you'd say. But he's nice. Oh yeah, and he has these humongous feet. I'm talking major feet, Momma. But nobody teases him about 'em."

"Why? Is he something special?"

Bobbie wondered how adults could be so ignorant sometimes. "Well, yeah, he's special. I just said. He's tall, and he's smart. You know."

"What did you say his name was?"

"Isaac Fellows." Down slipped the glasses.

Mrs. Ruffin got up to turn the chicken. As she lifted the lid, a cloud of spicy steam escaped into the room. "Ready soon," she observed, approving of the chicken's golden-brown crispness. "Looks like pretty decent chicken."

She switched the flame on under a pot of rice soaking in water, and sat back down. "Does this Isaac have anything to do with that gloomy face you've been pulling around here lately?"

"What gloomy face?" Bobbie tried to look cheerful and carefree.

Mrs. Ruffin wasn't buying it. "The gloomy face you put on before you leave this apartment in the morning," she answered.

Bobbie sighed. No matter what, the conversation got back on the same old track. And it led straight to The Myra Problem, the one problem she did not wish to discuss. As long as she didn't talk about it, she could pretend it didn't exist. And besides, she reminded herself, her mother had enough to worry about.

"It's not him," she said. Isaac sure wasn't the one who was giving her the blues.

"Then what is it?"

Geez, Bobbie thought, impatiently blowing a puff of air out of the corner of her mouth.

"You see?" Mrs. Ruffin complained to the ceiling. "My mind told me to ask this child about it this morning. But no, I was in too big a hurry trying to please that old turkey. For all the good it did me."

Bobbie's ears perked up. "Did Mr. Wigfall get

on your case again today, Momma?"

Mrs. Ruffin blinked. "Oh, that's not important, honey. Now getting back — "

"It's important to me." That was true. Her mother's happiness meant a lot to Bobbie.

"Well, he just — " Mrs. Ruffin began, her brow wrinkling. "I was a little late this morning, not more than a minute or two. I was all out of breath because like an idiot I took some of the steps two at a time.

"But there he was, waiting, dangling that precious pocket watch of his. And this is how he looked at me." She squeezed together her eyes, nose, and mouth like a cross between the Grinch and Ebenezer Scrooge.

"Did he say anything, Momma?"

"He said, 'Ah . . . Mrs. Ruffin. Ah . . . Did we lose our way this morning, hmmmmmm?' " She could mimic old Wigfall to a tee.

"So what did you say, Momma?" Bobbie demanded, angry at the insult to her mother.

Mrs. Ruffin looked surprised and a bit embarrassed at the question. "Well, I — I didn't say anything."

"You didn't? Why not?"

"Well, he's the principal, Bobbie."

Bobbie let her eyes drop. Except for the sounds of the sizzling chicken and the gently drizzling rain, the kitchen was quiet.

Mrs. Ruffin finally broke in with a thin laugh. "Wait a minute, here," she said, folding up her newspaper. "We were talking about you, as I recall. Remember? The girl with the gloomy face?"

Bobbie looked up. All this stuff was starting to crowd her: Myra, not having friends, and the showdown. And now some old coot dumping on her mom. She could feel it all welling up inside her and, before she could force it back down, it spilled down her cheeks.

Mrs. Ruffin reached for Bobbie. "Hey, hey now. Dry down those tears, little girl," she coaxed gently, wiping Bobbie's cheeks with her sleeve. "What's all this?"

"You let him say that to you and you didn't even say anything back!" Bobbie blurted out, salty tears on her tongue.

Her mother stroked her hair for a while before she answered. "You're right, I didn't," she said in a low voice.

"Just because he's the principal?"

This time Mrs. Ruffin's eyes dropped. "Because I was afraid to."

Afraid to, Bobbie repeated to herself. *Afraid.* Her mother. Something was all wrong here. Her mother always looked life straight in the eye. Like she did when things went bad with Bobbie's dad. Or when they had to move here, away from their whole family.

The rice began to boil and bubble, pushing the lid up and streaming down the side of the pot. Mrs. Ruffin got up again and turned the flame down.

"Times are really tough, sweetie. You know I was lucky to find this job," she said quietly, her back to Bobbie. "I'm still what they call provisional. Wigfall's the one who decides if I become part of the permanent staff."

But what about dignity? Bobbie was outraged. "You just can't let him do you like that, Momma! I'm going down there tomorrow! I'll tell him what's gonna happen to him if he keeps bothering you! I'll snatch that stupid pocket watch and — "

"Wait a minute, wait a minute!" Mrs. Ruffin turned around, the pot of rice still in hand. "You know I appreciate it, darlin', but you can't do that for me."

"Why not?" Bobbie pressed. She could see Wigfall now, his bald head bowed low, begging for mercy.

"Well, in the first place he just might know karate," Mrs. Ruffin quipped, trying to make Bobbie laugh. Then she put the pot down and looked serious. "In the second place, knucklehead, I'm the only one who can stand up for me."

Bobbie felt a tingle; she thought back to how she'd peeked over Isaac's shoulder while he took on Myra at the park.

"What's wrong with someone helping you out, like a friend or somebody?" she asked, trying not to give away too much.

"I'd say that was a nice friend, but I'd still have to do it myself."

"Why?"

"Because . . ." her mother said, concentrating, ". . . because my friend couldn't always be there. Sooner or later I'd have to face Wigfall by myself.

"And," she added, her eyes on Bobbie, "because I don't want my little girl to be ashamed of me."

"I'm not ashamed of you, Momma," Bobbie said softly. But she wanted some assurance that Wigfall was going to get his. "So why don't you just do it? Stand up for yourself, I mean."

Mrs. Ruffin thought for a minute. "I guess I better, hmmmmmmmmm?" she answered in her best Wigfall/Grinch voice.

Bobbie nodded, a little smile sneaking in.

"And, oh yes, by the way," Mrs. Ruffin asked offhandedly, "when are *you* going to do it?"

"Do what?" Bobbie asked, caught off guard.

"Stand up for *your*self."

Bobbie wasn't ready to answer. She was silent for so long that, worried about burning it, her mother turned back to tend the chicken. Then, without a word, Bobbie got up and grabbed her momma tightly around the waist.

"It's hard for me, too, sugar," Mrs. Ruffin whispered, pulling Bobbie close. "But we'll handle it. Right?"

Bobbie watched the raindrops hesitate at the top of the windowpane, then zigzag down to the puddle waiting somewhere down below. *Right*, she thought.

8

Some of the faces in the hall next morning had been at the park the day before. Bobbie watched for smirks, winks, giggles, hostility. But except for Myra's groupies, there was little more than curiosity mixed with guilt in the faces she saw. Some even nodded or waved in an almost friendly way. Yesterday is over, the feeling seemed to be. Today is another day.

In fact, the one face Bobbie had been on the lookout for was not there that morning. Myra hadn't been crouching in her usual ambush spot at the gate. She hadn't lurked in the hall, nor on the fringes of the basketball court where Isaac liked to practice.

Last night's rain had spent itself and left a fresh blue morning in its place. Looking good. Bobbie guessed happily that Myra would be absent. Her spirits lifting, she headed for Mrs. Schnurr's classroom. But she didn't go in.

Someone was standing outside the door, blocking her way. Someone about five feet two inches tall and in a wicked-evil mood.

"You know, one of these times Isaac ain't gonna be around to guard your skinny little behind." Myra was dressed for battle in a loud red plaid skirt, a fringed blue jeans jacket, and jump-shot high-top sneakers. Her hair was pulled up and away from her eyes, all the better to stare people down.

Bobbie could hear the pulse in her temples. Her knees wanted to quit on her. But she fought the urge to flee like a true Priss. *Come on, Roberta,* she pleaded. *Show some guts.*

The next thing Bobbie heard was a voice that sounded like her own. Shaky, but definitely her own.

"Move outta my way, Myra," the voice said.

Myra's mouth dropped wide open. So did Bobbie's. Neither girl could believe what she had just heard.

It had to happen, Bobbie thought. *I've gone insane. I just heard myself tell Myra Collins to move outta the way. That's it. My mind is gone.*

Myra shut her mouth. Throwing her hands onto her hips, planting her sneakers, and squenching her eyes into angry little slits, she spit out the dare.

"Make me."

By now the stream of students heading into the classroom had slowed into a puddle of nosy onlookers outside the door. Roland, always ready to witness some action, pushed his way to the front.

"Make me move, Bones," Myra repeated.

Big beads of sweat popped out on Bobbie's nose, and her glasses began sliding downwards. She knew the ball was in her court; she felt the eyes of the universe focused on her and her skidding eyeglasses.

"M-make you m-move?" she stammered, stalling. These things couldn't be rushed. Somebody's bones could get crunched. She searched the crowd for Isaac's stern face, but of all days, he wasn't there yet.

Myra had noticed that detail, too. "You heard me, stuck-up, glass-eye bag a' bones. MAKE ME MOVE." She stacked herself squarely between Bobbie and the door. There she loomed, hands on hips, mocking, large.

Think, Bobbie ordered herself. *If you panic, you're finished.* Her brain raced, her heart raced, and suddenly, it came to her.

Facing Myra head on, Bobbie slowly raised her eyes to the space above the taller girl's head. A relieved smile spread across her face.

"Good morning, Mrs. Schnurr," Bobbie said

sweetly, her gaze still fixed above Myra's head. "Just coming in."

Myra paused. Her parents had warned her to stay off Mrs. Schnurr's "Bad Actors" list; they would swarm all over her if she brought home another "U" in citizenship. She spun around to see where the teacher was. There was no one behind her, no one at all.

Just that quickly, Bobbie stepped around her and safely into the classroom. "You said to make you move," she called lightly over her shoulder. "You didn't say how to do it."

Led by Roland, the crowd of spectators by the door erupted into laughter.

"Wow! She got you, Myra!" Roland hooted, poking her in the ribs with his elbow. "Oldest trick in the book!"

"She faked Myra all the way out!" chimed in another.

"Didn't know she had the nerve . . ."

Bobbie made a beeline for her table. The bell was about to ring and she wanted to be well clear of Myra. Once seated at her familiar graffiti-pocked station, she noticed her trembling hands and quickly sat on them, thinking, *Did I actually tell Myra to move outta the way? Was that me?*

Feeling better by the minute, she answered herself. *YES!*

It wasn't long before she felt good, really good. She put her hands on top of her desk. They had stopped twitching. She looked around and caught Roland's eye. He winked at her, made a funny face, and broke himself up. A couple of girls near her, Gina and Jenna, smiled encouragingly. For the first time since she'd come to Lowell, Bobbie felt like a real warm-blooded being, not just a shadow.

The class session flew by. Bobbie flung her hand in the air every single time she knew the answer. Today, she wasn't worried about being singled out as a know-it-all. Today she cared little about hearing someone snicker "Snobby Bobbie" behind her back. She felt she was wearing some kind of radiant armor that shielded her from sticks, stones, and names that once had hurt her.

I didn't back down, she thought proudly. *I made her move. Me. Bobbie Bones.*

There were a few times during class when only two hands reached for the air. Hers and Isaac's. He, of course, extended only his index finger. Cooler that way.

Once, when they both knew the answer, she looked over at him. He sat back and folded his arms. "You take it, Miss B," he obliged her, smiling his most confident, most cool smile. The whole class was watching, fascinated.

Flustered, Bobbie almost forgot the answer altogether. Her head felt steamy, like a baked potato straining at the skin. But she stammered out the whole thing. And it was correct. And no one made a crack.

Isaac smiled at her again.

9

Eleven forty-five came suddenly that morning. Bobbie was amazed. Usually, the hand on the big, bold-faced clock ticked and ticked but never seemed to budge. Eleven forty-five it was, though, and she could already hear the screams and clamor of the other classes crowding the lunch tables outside the auditorium, near Mrs. Schnurr's window.

Mrs. Schnurr always insisted on two single-file lines all the way out the door and down the steps to the lunch tables. That's why her class always got there last.

This was a major sore point with Roland, whose stomach started grumbling and growling at 11:43 A.M. on the dot. He was usually sitting in The Pit — right by the window. From there he could easily see the other students getting to the tables on time and opening up fragrant ham sandwiches, bags of crisp potato chips, steaming thermoses of chicken and rice soup, pita bread stuffed with cheese.

"Ohhhh," Roland would groan. He couldn't make sense when he saw food. "Ohh, aw. . . . ohhhh . . ."

Finally, the lines would be assembled and Mrs. Schnurr would let Roland out of The Pit. It was always the best moment of his day.

And one of Bobbie's worst. It meant finding her place at the end of Room 12's table and sitting like a shadow through a lunch period with no table talk, no kidding around, no sandwich swapping.

But, even so, the sun felt good today. It was warm, but not too warm, bright but not too bright. And Bobbie had seen her mother spreading strawberry jam on her peanut buttered bread the night before, just the way she liked it, "Easy on the peanut butter, heavy on the jam."

She knew there were seedless grapes in there, too — the sweet, tight, not-quite-purple ones that crunched and popped between your molars. On top of all that, she had a new library book to start. So lunch was going to be just fine, table talk or no table talk.

"Can we squeeze in here?"

Bobbie looked up and squinted into the sun's glare, trying to focus.

"We usually sit at the end, but Roland's lunch

is spread out all over," the voice went on.

"You know what he has today?" asked a second voice. "That boy has the biggest burrito I ever saw. It looks like a suitcase. Check it out! Plus, his granma packed him *sardines!*"

"That's really why we decided to move," explained Voice Number One. "Can you scoot over?"

Bobbie had focused. It was Gina and Jenna, already gently shoving in on either side of her. She was so surprised she forgot she was two bites into her peanut butter sandwich, which she held in midair. Gina and Jenna always hung out together, but they'd never said much more to Bobbie than "Pass the chalk, please."

Now here they were, chatting away left and right. It was a miracle.

"Bobbie." It was Gina, her plump cinnamon-colored face blessed with perfect dimples.

It sounded strange to Bobbie to hear her name called by a classmate. She looked at Gina, eyes blinking.

"Your mouth is open," Gina said.

Bobbie shut it so quickly she almost bit her tongue. The two girlfriends laughed. But it was good laughter. Bobbie swallowed and chuckled at herself.

"So, don't you talk outside of class?" Jenna asked. Jenna was lanky and wore bangs that shot out over her forehead like a diving board. Between her two front teeth she had a friendly gap that made her smile irresistible.

"Yes," Bobbie said quickly. "I talk all the time. At my old school I used to talk too much — "

"You?" Jenna raised her eyebrows.

"Sure, me." Bobbie shrugged. "But here . . . nobody seems too interested."

"We thought *you* weren't interested," pitched in Gina, dimpling. "You never say anything to anybody. Except maybe Isaac."

"Well, he's the only one who talks to me. And I didn't know anybody."

"Well, we didn't know *you*!" Gina insisted.

"We thought you were snobby," Jenna added.

Bobbie cringed. The pain of the "Snobby Bobbie" name came creeping back.

"We heard about the little commotion at the park — " Jenna rushed on, fishing a drumstick out of her lunch bag.

" — but we didn't really know what happened," Gina finished. "Except that Isaac was on your side."

Bobbie wanted to forget the park. "It was . . . a little problem I've been having, with . . ."

"With Myra?" Gina said in a lower voice.

Bobbie nodded.

"Yeah. You know," Jenna volunteered in a

whisper, "she likes Isaac. And she's mad because he likes somebody else." The drumstick was growing skinnier by the minute.

Bobbie stared. "So you mean you think she thinks — "

"We're sure she thinks — "

"Positive — "

" — that Isaac likes you!"

"A lot!" Gina dimpled happily.

Bobbie forgot her sandwich again. In fact, it could have grown little peanut feet and run away without getting her attention.

"Bobbie?" Gina said.

Bobbie looked up.

"Your mouth is open again."

"Wide open," Jenna added as the three girls laughed together.

Jenna and Gina soon discovered Bobbie's not-quite-purple-seedless-crunch grapes and proved themselves serious traders. Jenna had a pear so hard she couldn't bite it head on; she had to go at it sideways, and even then it was like gnawing on a stone. Gina only had a tomato with a split skin. Somehow, each of the three wound up with a handful of grapes, a fractured piece of pear, and a pile of runny tomato. But everybody was happy.

Most of all Bobbie. Her two new friends told her they had seen her step around Myra that morning. It had opened their eyes.

"I probably would've just run the other way," Gina admitted.

"Behind me," seconded Jenna, between grapes.

But they agreed that Bobbie had handled herself well. It had been a victory for the Underdog Club, of which they were president, vice president, and entire membership.

"Now you can be second vice president," Gina said generously, "if you wanna be."

Bobbie beamed. Her hand went up. "I vote for me!"

They all laughed again, saluting each other with their juice cartons.

The sight of unfinished food caught Roland's eye, from his vantage point at the other end of the table. His sardines were history, as were his crackers, oranges, fruit roll-ups, boiled egg, sliced cheese, doughnuts, and peach pie. All he had left was a burrito big enough to ride home on. He cleared away his debris and sauntered over to the girls. Or, rather, to their food.

"Those are those crunchy grapes, huh?" he asked by way of greeting. "I could hear you crunchin' and munchin' way over there."

The girls kept munching. The grapes were great.

"Whose grapes?" he persisted, eyeing the fruit greedily. Red grapes were a favorite of his.

"These are Bobbie's grapes," Jenna told him. "But she's sharing with *us*."

Roland peered at Jenna's stash. "What's yours?"

"The rest of this pear," Jenna replied, suspiciously. "Why?"

"Man, it takes more than my granma packs to fill me up," Roland complained, shoving in next to Jenna. "If I had a pear or some grapes, my stomach wouldn't cut up all through social studies. Sure wish I had some pear."

"You can have some tomato, Roland," Gina dimpled sweetly, trying not to giggle. She pushed a heap of her split tomato over to him on a baggie.

"If I eat the tomato, can I have the pear?" he bargained. Roland was never proud about food.

The girls nodded their permission. He went through the little pile of squooshed tomato in two seconds, then reached for Jenna's remaining pieces of pear.

"I should warn you —" Jenna began.

Too late. Roland popped the whole piece into his mouth. His eyes went buggy when he tried to bite down.

"This thing is hard as a rock!" He pulled the offending fruit out, feeling betrayed.

"I tried to tell you, Roland!" Jenna scolded.

"What else you got?" he insisted, down but not out. He looked bewildered when Jenna, Gina, and Bobbie broke out in fresh giggles. To Roland, nothing was more serious than food.

"You trying to wipe out the world food supply, man?" a new voice cut in.

Bobbie and the other Underdogs looked way up. Isaac stood there, grinning at Roland. "You could start on that fat boy burrito in your pocket."

Roland shook his head. "I'm just trying to get full," he explained gravely. "This burrito's my insurance in case nothin' else turns up."

"Boy, Roland," Isaac laughed, joined by the chorus of three. He pulled out a treasure from his own sack: a chocolate cupcake, the kind with the creamy center.

Roland lunged at the cupcake like it was trying to get away. "Let me help you out with that," he offered Isaac, who surrendered the tidbit without a quarrel. He knew Roland would wind up with it anyway.

Bobbie was aware that Gina and Jenna were slyly trading glances, eyes darting between her and Isaac. They kept nudging each other, with "told you so" written all over their faces. She felt her glasses slipping down on her nose.

Pushing them up, her own glance fell on the corner where Myra held court at lunchtime. She looked away quickly; Myra was giving the five of them her undivided attention. Bobbie tried to ignore her, but Myra was not to be ignored.

Except by Isaac, who paid her no mind at all. He looked at Bobbie.

"You need nose pads," he advised her.

"Beg pardon?" Bobbie forced herself not to look in Myra's direction. She was nervous enough, now that Isaac had joined their group.

"Nose pads," he repeated, teasing, "to keep your bifocals from sliding down all the time."

Jenna and Gina chortled good-naturedly, but Bobbie felt flustered.

"They're not bifocals," she started to tell him, but the five-minute bell drowned her out. It was already time to start clearing away and file back into class. The time had zipped by.

"I'll dump the trash," she suggested, eager to do something for her new buddies. Gina and Jenna quickly loaded her up.

"We'll wait for you, Bobbie." They hung around the lunch table with the two boys.

It was a short trip across the square to the big trash can, but Bobbie had to weave her way through the noisy crush of students. She also had to pass by Big Myra, who had gotten up to clear away her own trash. Bobbie squeezed past her without turning her head.

She reached the can and dumped what was left

of their lunches. From the corner of her eye, she thought she saw Myra coming up fast on her right. There was no exit through the press of pushing bodies on her left, but she thrust her body forward anyway, trying to make a path in a hurry.

"Not that way, Miss Priss," a voice hissed in her ear. "This way!"

Bobbie suddenly felt a strong hand on her arm, pushing her sideways off balance, right into the big open garbage can. The can tipped over and crashed down with her, dumping the day's sour-smelling debris all over her head and upper body.

For a moment, Bobbie lay dazed in a heap of paper bags, apple cores, orange rind, and corn chips. Warm milk dripped cloudy tears down her cheeks. Something cold had smacked her on the neck, and she reached up warily to remove it. Like a giant purple Leech from the Unknown, a sticky fruit roll-up had attached itself there. She shuddered, peeled it off, and tried to focus.

Oh, no! Her heart sank. Focusing was going to be impossible. Her glasses were buried in that mess somewhere.

Gina and Jenna pushed through the crowd to rescue Bobbie, followed by Isaac and Roland.

"Get her glasses, Roland!" Isaac commanded, helping Bobbie struggle to her feet. The Underdogs got busy brushing chips off her sweatshirt, plucking raisins out of her hair, wiping her sour milk tears. Not much they could do about the smeared peanut butter.

Roberta Mavis Ruffin was a smelly, drippy, *bona fide* catastrophe.

Under all that garbage, she felt her face burning with shame. As hot tears rose in her eyes, she tried to blink back the flood. She could not cry, she told herself. She would not cry. But the tears broke through and washed down her face.

Just when things were going great, she wailed to herself. *Just look at me! What are they going to think now?*

She was glad she couldn't see too well. The bell had rung, but a good many of her classmates were still milling around, aware there was a disaster going on here. Bobbie wanted to hide from them. Their faces were a blur to her, but she was sure they must be laughing like crazy. How many girls do you see wearing fruit roll-up on their necks?

Roland located her glasses down in the muck, a little gooey but unbroken. "Here you go," he said gallantly, dangling them by the frame and holding his nose. Bobbie, still reeling a little, muttered her thanks and tried to wipe the glasses with the limp paper napkin Gina handed her.

She pushed them up on her nose and took a hapless look around, delicately holding her splattered sweatshirt away from her skin.

Right away, she spotted Myra back in her corner. Arms folded, she was looking on with amusement.

Bobbie thought of the hissing voice in her ear, of the push, the fall, the fruit roll-up plastered on her neck. She looked again at Myra, who snorted and made a crack to her neighbor.

That did it. Bobbie's anger sprang up like a panther in her blood.

"Bobbie wait a second — " shouted Gina, snatching at her friend's soggy sleeve as Bobbie shot past her. It was too late. Bobbie Bones was *mad.*

10

Myra's red plaid skirt was the biggest target in the lunch area. It was the only one Bobbie needed to make out through her smeared glasses. Boiling with anger, she grabbed the first thing her hand fell on: Roland's Big Boy Burrito.

She dashed over to Myra's camp, drew back, and prepared to fire the burrito with all her might.

But a hand clutched her wrist and held firm. "Bad idea, Miss B."

She spun around, breathing hard through her mouth. It was Isaac. Still holding her wrist with one great paw, he managed with the other to remove the burrito from Bobbie's clenched fist. Roland scampered over and retrieved his precious "insurance," relieved that it was his again.

Bobbie saw purple. "Give me back that burrito!" she demanded. "I'm gonna — I'm gonna — "

"Get yourself in a lot of trouble," Isaac finished for her. "Here comes the Shnoo."

True enough. Mrs. Schnurr was on the case, descending at full speed upon the group. Mrs. Marshall, the vice principal, was close by. Double trouble.

"What's going on here? What's going on here?" they were asking everyone, pushing their way through the crowd. They soon spied Bobbie, in all her sour milk and soggy glory, and came to a full stop.

"Bobbie!" Mrs. Schnurr gasped. "My heavens, what in the world happened to you? Are you hurt?"

Bobbie shook her head. She wanted to crawl back under the trash can and just quietly ferment.

Mrs. Marshall, an expert in schoolyard "accidents," looked poor Bobbie up and down. Her eyes then swept the crowd, coming to rest on Big Myra Collins. Myra tried to look innocent; she stepped politely back from the crowd and began to study the clouds scudding in the serene blue sky.

Turning back to Bobbie, Mrs. Marshall's voice was razor-sharp. "Who's responsible for this, Roberta?"

Bobbie's sticky glasses were sitting lopsided again. She pushed them to the right, then to the left. She took them off and tried wiping them on her soaked sleeve. She wanted to be at home, on her bed, with her critters who never pushed her into trash cans. She wanted her momma.

If only Isaac would just handle it. But he was silent, like everyone else.

"Roberta," Mrs. Marshall urged.

Bobbie did not look up. She was sure that if she did, she would look straight at the guilty party. She bit her lip, her anger rushing out like a tide of boiling waves, leaving her drained and tired.

Mrs. Marshall and the others waited. Finally, Bobbie gave her answer.

"I'm okay, Mrs. Marshall. It must've been an accident," she said, eyes still down.

"What? An accident?" Mrs. Marshall repeated. "Come on, now. Did you fall or were you pushed?"

"I'm okay, Mrs. Marshall," Bobbie insisted feebly. "Really, I'm okay. It won't happen again. Really."

Around the lunch area, students murmured under their breath. They studied Bobbie respectfully. She was no shadow now and never would be again.

Mrs. Marshall's sharp eyes picked Myra out of the crowd. "It better not," she warned, grimly.

Then, all business, she bustled order back into the scene. "Now, you students go to your rooms. Mrs. Schnurr, I'll take Roberta to the office so she can call her mother. She can't hang around here smelling like a garbage truck."

The students fell over themselves trying to follow Mrs. Marshall's orders. She had that effect on people. Bobbie almost had to skip to keep up with the woman's rapid march-step.

Gina and Jenna hurried alongside their fellow Underdog. "You coulda nailed her," Jenna whispered breathlessly. "You let her off scot-free!"

Gina dimpled with pride. "Everybody's saying you're — just — the best!"

Still half-skipping, Bobbie stared at the two girls. She was astonished. "Me? They're saying. . . ?"

Gina nodded vigorously. "Are you coming back to school after you change clothes?"

Bobbie flashed an elated smile. "I'll be back," she assured them, disappearing into Mrs. Marshall's office.

The table area was nearly clear of the lunch bunch. Myra had hung back deliberately, making sure that Mrs. Marshall had really marched away. She looked around and found herself just about deserted. Those few kids remaining looked at her strangely before clamoring up the steps into the building. Myra slowly headed for the steps, kicking a stray apple core.

Someone was passing her on the steps. Finishing off the last of the Big Boy Burrito and licking his fingers, Roland grinned at Myra. "Looks like Bobbie Bones gotcha again, huh Myra?"

Myra pretended to ignore Roland's glee. She stared straight past him into the gloom of the hallway, full of students pushing their way into the Shnoo's classroom. She caught a glimpse of Isaac's straight back, fading into the noisy throng.

When she walked into the room, the air seemed chilly.

11

The hot steam rising from her tub water soothed Bobbie more than usual. There was something luxurious about a bath in the middle of the day, even to wash off garbage-can gunk. She let her toes peek above the water and pretended she was Queen Nefertiti, waiting for someone to pour rare perfumes into her bathing pool.

Instead, Mrs. Ruffin came in, fussing. "If you plan to get back to school today, you'd better hustle, honey doll," she said, pinching Bobbie's soiled sweatshirt between two fingers and pitching it into the hamper.

"Whoo!" She wrinkled her nose. "We may have to bury this stuff!"

She glanced at her watch. "Actually, Bobbie, you may as well stay home now. You'd have less than an hour of class left by the time you got back. My day is almost over anyway, so I could call in — "

"No, Momma! I'm hurrying!" Bobbie broke in, scrubbing herself with a fury. "I told Gina and Jenna I'd be back."

"Gina Jenna? Who's Gina Jenna?"

"Gina *and* Jenna. Two girls in my class. We made friends today," Bobbie added, shyly fighting back a grin.

A bright beam crossed Mrs. Ruffin's face. "Well!" she exclaimed, pushing everything else aside and sitting down on the side of the tub. "So tell me."

Bobbie told her about lunchtime and Gina and Jenna and the Underdogs. She left out the part about Isaac liking her. She was still whirling over that.

When she finished, her mother kept her seat on the tub. "That's great, kiddo!" she said, delighted. "So that's the good news. What about the bad news?"

Bobbie looked at her innocently. "The bad news?"

"Come on," Mrs. Ruffin folded her arms. "About how you got dumped on. Mrs. Marshall just said you had a little accident, and you'd tell me what happened."

Bobbie splashed noisily and pulled the plug out of the drain hole. "Oh. Well, you know, it was an accident, like she said." She stood up, reached for her towel, and began to rub herself dry.

Mrs. Ruffin let a minute or two go by, her arms still folded. "Okay, you can stop rubbing," she said when Bobbie started in on the spaces between her toes. "You are dry, kiddo. Now start talking."

Bobbie knew she was cornered. Sooner or later her mother would worm it out of her anyway. She sighed and told the tale as quickly as she could: the hissing in her ear, the push, the fall, her refusal to tell on Myra.

Her mother listened, nodding, until Bobbie finished. Then she got up, went to the sink, and soaked a facecloth in cold water. "This Myra," she said, wringing out the cloth and pressing it to her face. "Big girl, huh?"

Bobbie described her.

"Will she come at you again?"

"I don't know," Bobbie answered. "Knowing Myra, she probably will." Bobbie pulled on a fresh yellow sweatshirt and stepped into a pair of clean jeans. The thought of facing Myra again did not make her happy.

"What are you going to do?" Mrs. Ruffin's voice was a little muffled by the damp cloth.

Bobbie's smile was forlorn. "Call the exterminator, I guess."

"I see," Mrs. Ruffin said with a straight face. "The exterminator. Nah, that's no good. They probably charge too much."

Geez, Bobbie shook her head with a tolerant

smile. Her mother could crack some really pitiful jokes.

"But wait a minute." Mrs. Ruffin put the cloth down and, eyes bright, looked straight at Bobbie. "I know somebody who can give you some good advice. For free."

"Who?" Bobbie asked doubtfully.

"*You*, knucklehead," Mrs. Ruffin replied. "I took it myself today, and dadgum if it didn't work."

Bobbie looked curious.

"You see," Mrs. Ruffin explained with relish, "Old Wigfall decided to embarrass me in the faculty meeting this afternoon. He'd gone and added up all the minutes I've been late this year. He was so proud of himself!

"So he walks over to my chair. 'My, my. Twelve and a half minutes of tardy time. Tsk, tsk, tsk. How do we plan to make up all these minutes, Mrs. Ruffin, hmmmmmmmmmm?'

"Nobody says a word. Finally, he says to me, 'Well, Mrs. Ruffin?'

"So I stood up. I said, 'I work late here every day free of charge, Mr. Wigfall. You got your twelve and a half minutes back a long time ago, sir. But you wouldn't know that. You see, you're out of here five minutes before the two-thirty bell rings every day.' "

They laughed as Mrs. Ruffin described the principal's face twitching as he searched for something to say.

"Weren't you scared to say that to him, Momma?" Bobbie asked.

"Yes I was, at first," Mrs. Ruffin admitted. "But once I stood up, it was me and him, Jim!" She snapped her fingers and tossed her head in triumph.

"And you won," Bobbie exulted.

"Well, let's just say he backed off," her mother said, calming down some. "So you see it was good advice. Maybe you should take it yourself, hmmmmmmmmmmmmm?"

Bobbie grinned. Standing beside her mother, she peered into the mirror at their reflections. She had never noticed before that they held their heads the same way. With their chins tilted up, ever so slightly.

"Good gosh, look at the time!" Mrs. Ruffin yelled suddenly, snatching up her purse. "If we're going back to school today, we better move it, Buster! Let's roll!"

No sooner had Mrs. Schnurr uttered the class' favorite phrase — "You may go, class" — than Jenna and Gina headed straight for Bobbie's table. Her self-appointed honor guard, they escorted her out of the classroom. Bobbie felt pleased and happy, part of the picture at last.

"Hey, the Underdogs are going to be the hottest group in the fifth grade," Jenna predicted. "The hottest, honey. Just wait."

The three comrades walked arm in arm through the hall, returning the respectful greetings of the other kids. The newest Underdog had shown the world she had a large and noble heart. The other two were proud to let a little of her glory shine on them as well.

Gina and Jenna had to leave Bobbie in the yard. They both took the bus and, as usual, they had to run for it. "See you tomorrow!" they called. "Don't forget we have to get your phone number!"

"Okay!" Bobbie yelled as they shot away, braids flapping and book bags slapping their sides. "See you tomorrow!"

Bobbie watched them pile into the bus and wave out of the window. As the bus pulled off, she waved back and stood still, glowing.

Turning towards the gate, she saw Isaac running to catch up with her. As he got closer, though, he downshifted into a casual stroll.

"Hey," he greeted her, dribbling his ball.

"Hi, Isaac." Bobbie was so glad she'd changed into her butter-yellow sweatshirt. Yellow looked good on brown skin, she'd heard Aunt Mave tell her mother once. For once, she had to agree with good old Aunt Mave.

Isaac reached into his pocket and produced a

little package. "Here," he said, holding the package in his outstretched palm.

Curious, Bobbie took it. It was a pair of nose pads for her eyeglasses.

"I don't need 'em," Isaac explained, looking at the sky. "You can have 'em. They keep your bifocals from, you know, sliding down all the time."

"Thank you, Isaac," Bobbie said softly. "They're beautiful." *Oh, man!* she cringed. *How could you call a nose guard beautiful, you dummy?!*

"Right," Isaac shrugged, as if reading her thought. "Forget it. No big thing." He started to dribble away to the court, where Roland and the other boys were waiting and beckoning to him. But after a couple of dribbles, he stopped and turned around.

"Want me to walk you home?"

Bobbie had to look down. The ground under her feet had transformed itself into a rising cloud, and she felt herself helplessly floating.

Her voice trembled a bit. "That's all right. They're waiting for you," she said, glancing over at Roland's round form jumping up and easily sinking sensational three-point shots . . . with no ball. "Maybe I can stay and watch you play a little tomorrow. If that would be okay?"

Isaac answered by spinning the ball on his index finger. "See you tomorrow, Miss B."

Bobbie watched him lope away on his big flopping feet. Amazing, she mused, how he could get around so easily on feet so . . . so. . . . But no matter. Who cared about feet anyway?

She sighed, smiling. Her cloud buoyed her gently, hovering above the ground she had walked on just the day before, when she had been a mere shadow.

One rotten day after another and then, poof! All of a sudden one of them turns golden right before your eyes, she marveled. But there it was. A golden shimmer washed the trees, the sky, the playground, even the dingy old brick school building.

Turning again towards the gate, she closed her eyes for a moment and clutched her book bag to her chest. She felt a part of the shimmering day, at one with the green rustling trees, the soft warm air.

When Bobbie opened her eyes, the daydream disintegrated. Big Myra stood at the gate, waiting for her.

12

This time, Myra waited alone. Bobbie observed absentmindedly how different she looked without her usual troop. She looked smaller, and not as menacing. Still, one had to be careful. No need to be pushy. Gingerly, Bobbie started through the gate.

"Hey, girl." She heard the familiar mocking tone in Myra's voice, but kept going, concentrating on the gate.

"I said, *hey*, girl." Myra stepped into her path.

Bobbie's feet slammed on the brakes. Okay, this was it. *You're the only one who can stand up for you*, she coached herself. *So do it. Do it.*

She hiccuped. *Gimme a break*, she thought, exasperated. *I can't have the hiccups now.* To stave off the next one, she sucked in all the air around her and held it until she felt dizzy.

Then, with a rush of exhaled breath, she spoke up.

"I heard you the first time, *girl*! Whaddayou want?" Bobbie was thrilled that her voice sounded feisty.

Myra paused, looking surprised at this show of spunk. Squinting one eye, she shot a keen dagger out of it, but Bobbie did not flinch.

The big girl, frustrated, stepped up close. "I'll tell you what I want, Thing. I want you to keep your bony little behind out of my way," she growled. "Grinnin' up in the teacher's face, trying to act like Miss Goody-Goody. You ain't slick."

She looked Bobbie up and down. "And you can forget about Isaac, baby, 'cause he's taken."

Hot wrath swept over Bobbie for the second time that day. Isaac had nothing to do with this! Not as far as she was concerned, anyway. She struggled for control, but her words began to spill out in a flood of anger and hurt.

"I don't grin up in the teacher's face!" she shouted, pushing up her glasses. "I don't grin up in anybody's face! That's just your excuse to pick on me!"

"Pick on you? Dream on, Bony," Myra shot back, coolly. "You ain't worth pickin' on. Stuck-up bag a' bones." She did not budge from the middle of the path.

Bobbie knew Myra could send her spinning at

any second. But her blood was up now. She decided to go for broke. Whatever was going to happen, let it happen now.

"I'm not stuck up, Myra, I'm just smart!" She flung the words out with a kind of relief. *Smart, yeah, and proud of it!* One look at Myra's face told her she had struck home.

But Bobbie's feelings were still coming out fast, tumbling one over the other. "The first day I came here you decided you didn't like me. Okay. But I can't push a button and turn my brain off just to please you! I am the way I am. And because of that, I've been the one on the outside. Until today."

Myra had stepped back a little. "Yeah, until today," she said, glaring. "Now we got three little Snobby Bobbies running around here."

"If you mean Jenna and Gina," Bobbie fumed, thrusting a shoulder forward, "they're not snobs! They're the first girls at this school who acted friendly to me. The rest of you just stuck your noses in the air.

"So if anyone around here is a snob, it's not me, and it's not Jenna and Gina. It's you!"

Myra was astonished. No one at Lowell had ever, ever called her that. She stood speechless, staring at Bobbie.

"Myra," Bobbie said quietly.

"What?" Myra responded automatically.

"Your mouth is open," Bobbie said. Myra shut it quickly and tried to regroup.

Bobbie's insides were churning like a washing machine, but she sensed that she was onto something. A look she had never seen had come into the big girl's eyes. It was plain that Myra was actually thinking things over.

Be quiet don't blow it, be quiet don't blow it, Bobbie chanted silently. The situation was very, very delicate.

All around them, the afternoon was still, except for the white and green waving birches planted outside the main building and by the gate. A gentle current of air rocked the trees back and forth, soothing and calm. Most of their schoolmates had long since tumbled on home. They were alone by the gate.

Hoping it was just the right moment, Bobbie made her move. *Now or never, Roberta Ruffin,* she reminded herself. She took a step towards Myra, not knowing exactly what she was going to do. Smile, maybe. Reach out, somehow.

But the noise of the boys' basketball game wafted towards them on the warm afternoon breeze. The sound of Isaac's voice pierced the air between them as they stood motionless by the gate.

Suddenly, Myra seemed to snap out of it. The scowl took over again, muscling out the new expression she'd worn the minute before. She turned on Bobbie and advanced, fist rolled up tight.

Bobbie's whole body yelled, *Here it comes! Run for your life!* She tried to think what it would take to get herself on the other side of that gate. Myra was filling up the path like a large boulder.

But Bobbie was frozen in place. Her feet had clutched on her. *So this is how it ends*, she thought dramatically. Shutting her eyes tightly and bracing herself, she stood her ground not eighteen inches from the outside gate and freedom.

Myra was so close Bobbie could hear her breathing. Hugging her books like a shield, she waited to defend her "you no what." She waited some more.

Finally, the suspense was too great. Bobbie cracked an eye.

Myra was hesitating. Still scowling, but hesitating. "You better run," she snarled. To make her point, she gave Bobbie a shove on the shoulder.

Bobbie stumbled but recovered.

"Run, Bony. This is your last chance." Myra shoved the shoulder again. "I said run!"

Bobbie was not going to run. She was Loretta

Ruffin's daughter, and, she thought proudly, Ruffins don't run. Besides, her feet were still locked in neutral.

Myra moved in for another shove. This time, Bobbie put her books up and blocked the shot.

"Don't do that again," she warned Myra. "I mean it." And she did. Like she had never meant anything before. For once, every skinny inch of her body stood ready to back her up. If it took all afternoon. That last shove from Myra had sent the old scary Bobbie tumbling right out of her.

Pushing her glasses way up on her nose, she looked Myra deep in the eye.

And then Bobbie knew there would be no battle that day. Or the next. They both knew it.

Slowly, Myra unballed her fist and shifted her feet. Watching Bobbie carefully, she stood back just far enough to let the girl pass through the gate.

"Nobody's thinkin' 'bout you, girl," she said to Bobbie's back.

Bobbie glanced around. "I'm not worried about it anymore, Myra."

She started for home. The trees nodded to her along the way, a green rustling nod of approval. "We told you good days were coming," they seemed to whisper to her.

Bobbie smiled at them. Little by little, her heaving chest quieted. She couldn't wait to tell her mother about this. The Ruffins were two for two today.

"Not bad," Loretta Ruffin would say with a wink, "for two skinny girls."

Filled with an excitement new to her, Bobbie picked up speed. The faster she went, the more her head cleared. The clearer her head, the more she felt the urge to look back.

So she looked. She saw Big Myra, still standing by the gate, alone. A wind came up and whipped her large red plaid skirt.

Bobbie looked ahead again. Now she felt a little sorry for Myra. She knew what it was like to be left alone.

Maybe they would even speak to each other tomorrow. Who could tell? Maybe they would even become good fri — well, at least not enemies.

She imagined herself generously helping Myra with her schoolwork. In her vision, Mr. and Mrs. Collins hovered nearby, serving them chocolate sundaes and smiling gratefully. Yes, anything was possible now.

Geez, maybe tomorrow would even be another good day.

Bobbie began to run. Her body felt light and lifting, with the wind. She felt free.

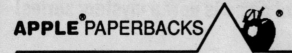

APPLE® PAPERBACKS

Pick an Apple and Polish Off Some Great Reading!

BEST-SELLING APPLE TITLES

☐ MT43944-8	Afternoon of the Elves	Janet Taylor Lisle	$2.75
☐ MT43109-9	Boys Are Yucko	Anna Grossnickle Hines	$2.95
☐ MT43473-X	The Broccoli Tapes	Jan Slepian	$2.95
☐ MT40961-1	Chocolate Covered Ants	Stephen Manes	$2.95
☐ MT45436-6	Cousins	Virginia Hamilton	$2.95
☐ MT44036-5	George Washington's Socks	Elvira Woodruff	$2.95
☐ MT45244-4	Ghost Cadet	Elaine Marie Alphin	$2.95
☐ MT44351-8	Help! I'm a Prisoner in the Library	Eth Clifford	$2.95
☐ MT43618-X	Me and Katie (The Pest)	Ann M. Martin	$2.95
☐ MT43030-0	Shoebag	Mary James	$2.95
☐ MT46075-7	Sixth Grade Secrets	Louis Sachar	$2.95
☐ MT42882-9	Sixth Grade Sleepover	Eve Bunting	$2.95
☐ MT41732-0	Too Many Murphys	Colleen O'Shaughnessy McKenna	$2.95

Available wherever you buy books, or use this order form.